In this story you will review the short vowel sounds. Can you find these words and sound them out?

this	**his**	**rag**	**box**	**all**	**fun**
is	**bed**	**doll**	**best**	**have**	**with**

Here are some sight words:

likes **of** **to**

Here are some fun words:

Biscuit **ball** **biscuits** **friends**

This is Biscuit.

Biscuit likes his bed.

Biscuit likes his ball.

Biscuit likes his rag doll.

Biscuit likes his
box of biscuits.

Best of all, Biscuit likes
to have fun with his friends!